THE MOST FOOLISH OF MEN

TAHIR SHAH

FAFANITTO

THE MOST FOOLISH OF MEN

A Teaching Story

TAHIR SHAH

FAFANITTO

MMXXIV

Secretum Mundi Publishing Ltd
124 City Road
London
EC1V 2NX
United Kingdom

www.secretum-mundi.com
info@secretum-mundi.com

First published by Secretum Mundi Publishing Ltd, 2024
A version of this story originally appeared in *Scorpion Soup* by Tahir Shah, 2013

THE MOST FOOLISH OF MEN

Artwork drawn by Fafanitto (Fateme Bagheri)

A CIP catalogue record for this title is available from the British Library.

ISBN 978-1-915876-12-6

VERSION 02052023

Visit the author's website:
Tahirshah.com

However brightly it sparkles, no diamond grows when planted in the ground.

Peruvian saying

Teaching Stories

When I was small, I was told stories from morning till night.

I was told stories about genies and witches and about great birds that could carry away elephants on their wings... and stories about distant kingdoms and magical lands ruled by warrior kings.

I was told stories of good and bad... stories of hope and others of despair.

I was even told stories about stories.

And all the while, I listened, amazed.

The more I listened, the more my mind worked... and the more I came to understand that these stories had a power about them, a secret lifeblood all of their own.

They were magical instruments, machineries that could alter states of mind and change the way we think.

But most importantly of all, stories can teach us, without us realizing that they are doing so at all.

Part of the default programming of man, stories are within us all.

Born into us, they make us who we are – they make us human.

Since earliest childhood, I have feasted on stories as a way of learning about the world, and learning about myself. They have been my dictionary and my encyclopaedia, my classroom, my guide, and my very best friend.

To descend down through the layers of stories is to be reborn, into a dominion of fantasy – one touched by real magic.

Pre-eminent within the great treasuries of tales, it is teaching stories like this one that have shown me the path to follow beyond the next horizon, and have made me the man I am.

Tahir Shah

There was once a king who
was loved by all his people.

On the day of his first son's birth,
a soothsayer was brought to the royal palace.

Bending over the royal crib, he declared that the infant would have a long and contented life, and would be adored by all.

‘But,’ the soothsayer added before going on his way, ‘the prince must never – in any circumstances – ever be bathed.’

The monarch threw up his hands in confusion.
'Why not?' he asked urgently.

‘Because, Your Majesty,’ the diviner replied, ‘he is prophesied to drown.’

Accordingly, throughout his childhood,
the royal prince was never bathed,
but rather sponged down from time to time.

A special department was established in the royal household to make sure that the prince's bath sponge never became too moist.

And when the boy drank liquid, guards watched very closely as the glass touched the royal lips.

The prince was kept away from
liquid of any kind.

Never permitted to get close to the water's edge at the river, or onto the beach down at the sea, he was protected in every conceivable way – his guards keeping a vigilant eye over their ward.

He was never shown a stream, a lake,
a waterfall, an icicle or snow…

… never permitted to swim,
or even to paddle his toes.

And when it rained, he was hastened inside
for fear that an unexpected inundation
might claim his life.

Years slipped by, and the prince grew up.

On the morning of his father's death,
he ascended the throne as king.

At last, he thought to himself,
I shall be able to take control of my destiny
and learn to swim.

Somehow sensing his enthusiasm for water, his mother, the widowed queen, stepped from the shadows and said:

‘Dearest son, I caution you to keep away from water. You know the soothsayer’s prediction. Will you promise me that you will abide by it?’

Sighing in agreement, the young man said:
'If it pleases you, dear Mother, I promise.'

And so yet more years slipped by, and the new king was blessed with children of his own and lived a long and just life.

With the passage of time,
he came to know old age.

In all the decades he had walked the earth and worn a crown, he had never once experienced the joy that water can bring.

Then, one day, the aged king
found it a little hard to breathe.

He called his chamberlain, and the chamberlain called the physician royal.

As he examined the monarch's chest,
the respected doctor prescribed a treatment.

But the treatment did not have a positive effect, and the king became all the more unwell.

Summoned to the regal bedside in the middle of the night, the physician royal examined the monarch once again.

‘What’s the matter with me?’ groaned the king.

His face fraught with worry,
the physician royal replied without thinking:

‘The trouble, Your Majesty, is that your lungs are filling with water – and you are drowning.’

Within a day, the king was dead,
and his eldest son was crowned king.

Despite the coronation, there was much tearing out of hair, and misery and grief.

Shrouds of mourning covered the buildings as the populace struggled to come to terms with their loss.

Their sorrow derived as much from the fact that the eldest son was an imbecile as it did from the passing of his father – an exemplary and popular king.

However hard he tried, the new ruler couldn't think of a way to relieve the sense of national sorrow.

To tell the truth, he couldn't really
think of anything much at all.

He was so stupid that his own family made jokes about his lack of intelligence when his back was turned, and they called him Nums, which was short for 'Numskull'.

Weeks and months went by,
and the people forgot how to smile.

After all, with an idiot on the throne,
there was nothing at all to smile about.

Then, one morning, the new young king had an idea.

He would create a diversion – a diversion
to take everyone's mind off the melancholy.

A contest, the winner of which would
be presented with fifty bags of gold.

‘What form shall the contest take,
O Imperial Majesty?’ asked the vizier.

The king thought for a long while.
'What do the people – *my* people
– love best of all?' he asked.

‘They love to be amused, Your Majesty.’

A grin slipped over the monarch's lips.
He began to giggle.

‘Then amusement they shall have!’
he exclaimed.

The next day, a herald criss-crossed the capital announcing the details of the contest:

'His Majesty the King will himself award fifty bags of gold to the stupidest person in the kingdom,' he cried. 'Anyone imagining themselves to be especially stupid may come to the royal palace tomorrow at dawn!'

All at once, the city seemed to erupt in excitement.

Wives pulled their husbands out of teahouses, calling: 'Come on, you idiot, you can earn us a fortune!' or 'You're the most foolish man I've ever met, you will surely win!'

Long before the sun had broken over the horizon, a snaking line of hopeful imbeciles wended its way through the streets and up to the palace gates.

BOW WOW

They included a man so stupid that he barked like a dog, and another who had a fork sticking out of his eye because he had missed his mouth by mistake.

One by one, they were admitted into the palace, where the vizier and his staff examined them.

Each contestant was permitted a full minute to demonstrate how stupid they were, after which most were kicked unceremoniously out of a side door and back onto the street.

A handful of applicants were
ordered to return at dusk.

Among them was a man who had married a broomstick thinking it was a beautiful woman, and an old crone who had raised a flock of pigeons, certain they were her children.

Just as the gates were about to be closed that evening, a young man called Mustafa arrived.

He was holding a package wrapped up in brown paper and string, and was whistling through his teeth.

'Are you sure that you're very stupid?'
asked the guard in a threatening tone.

Mustafa gave a salute.
'Of course I am,' he said. 'Get out my way,
for I am the King of Bukhara!'

‘Of course you are,’
replied the guard, waving him through.

Somehow, young Mustafa was mixed in with the line of finalists. He took his place on a chair, which he turned upside down before perching upon it.

When refreshments were brought round by an orderly, he poured them over his head and croaked like a frog.

CROAK

Eventually, the king swept into the throne room, ready to judge those who had made it through to the next round.

‘Who will be first to amuse me?’ he cried out.

The man with the fork in his eye
sloped into the throne room.

He was followed by a woman who
had married a clutch of kittens.

After them came a one-legged sailor
who hopped in backwards.

‘Who’s next?’ cried the vizier.

Mustafa found himself
pushed into the firing line.

'*Well*...?' said the king, bored by it all.
'How stupid are *you*?'

Pulling the brown-paper package out from behind his back, the young man said nothing.

Rather, he unwrapped the parcel,
revealing a mirror.

Stepping up to the throne, he held the mirror so that it reflected the king's face.

'You had wanted to see the stupidest man in the kingdom,' he said curtly, 'and now you can do just that!'

Everyone froze.

Silence prevailed for what seemed an eternity.

The vizier covered his mouth with a hand and prayed. The serving staff dared not breathe. The other contestants tiptoed out in terror.

Even the guards winced, fearful that their monarch would go wild with rage.

But Mustafa stood his ground.

The king stared at his visage
uneasily in the glass.

Then, slowly, he broke into a smile –
a smile that developed into a thunderous
roar of laughter.

'Award this man the prize of fifty bags of gold!' he boomed.

Finis

About the Author

Descended from a long line of storytellers, writers, and savants, Tahir Shah is one of the most prolific authors of his generation. He has published more than sixty books in numerous genres, including travel, fiction, and fantasy, as well as tales for children.

Raised in the tradition of Eastern 'teaching stories', Shah is passionate about stories and storytelling. He regards the ability to learn from folklore as being in us all, what he calls a 'default setting of humankind'. As well as having written scores of books, Shah has made documentaries for National Geographic TV and The History Channel. He is the founder and CEO of the charity, The Scheherazade Foundation.

About the Artist

Fateme Bagheri (Fafanitto) was born in Iran. She started learning to paint at the age of twelve, before gaining her bachelor's degree in painting at Alzahra University and then her master's in illustration at Tehran University. She draws her inspiration from traditional Persian art.

Books By Tahir Shah

The Writer's Craft

The Reason to Write

Workbook: Comprehensive, Volume I & II

Workbook: Fantasy, Volume I & II

Workbook: Fiction, Volume I & II

Workbook: Historical Fiction, Volume I & II

Workbook: Teaching Stories, Volume I & II

Workbook: Travel, Volume I & II

Novels

Jinn Hunter: Book One – The Prism

Jinn Hunter: Book Two – The Jinnslayer

Jinn Hunter: Book Three – The Perplexity

Hannibal Fogg and the Supreme Secret of Man

Casablanca Blues

Eye Spy

Godman

Paris Syndrome

Timbuctoo

Midas

Zigzagzone

Nasrudin

Travels With Nasrudin

The Misadventures of the Mystifying Nasrudin

The Peregrinations of the Perplexing Nasrudin

The Voyages and Vicissitudes of Nasrudin

Nasrudin in the Land of Fools

Travel

Trail of Feathers
Travels With Myself
Beyond the Devil's Teeth
In Search of King Solomon's Mines
House of the Tiger King
In Arabian Nights
The Caliph's House
Sorcerer's Apprentice
Journey Through Namibia

Teaching Stories

The Arabian Nights Adventures
Scorpion Soup
Tales Told to a Melon
The Afghan Notebook
Daydreams of an Octopus & Other Stories
The Caravanserai Stories
Ghoul Brothers
Hourglass
Imaginist
Jinn's Treasure
Jinnlore
Mellified Man
Skeleton Island
Wellspring
When the Sun Forgot to Rise
Outrunning the Reaper
The Cap of Invisibility
On Backgammon Time
The Wondrous Seed

The Paradise Tree
Mouse House
The Hoopoe's Flight
The Old Wind
A Treasury of Tales
The Tale of Double Six
The Forgotten Game
King of the Jinns
The Destiny Ring
Changing the World
Cat, Mouse
Frogland
Mittle-Mittle
Capilongo
The Princess of Zilzilam
The Singing Serpents
The Tale of the Rusty Nail
The Unicorn's Tear
The Clockmaker Who Travelled Through Time
The Fish's Dream
The Man Whose Arms Grew Branches
The Most Foolish of Men
The Shop That Sold Truth
Qwerty
Renaissance
The Man With the Tiger's Head
The Kingdom of Blink
The Wisdom of Celestine
Dream Soup
The Skeleton Factory
An Unexpected Gift

The Problem Exchange
The Pharaoh Code
The Monkey Puzzle Club
Liquid Time
Cat Dog, Dog Cat
Princess Pickle's Laugh

Anthologies

The Anthologies: Africa
The Anthologies: Ceremony
The Anthologies: Childhood
The Anthologies: City
The Anthologies: Danger
The Anthologies: East
The Anthologies: Expedition
The Anthologies: Frontier
The Anthologies: Hinterland
The Anthologies: India
The Anthologies: Jinns
The Anthologies: Jungle
The Anthologies: Magic
The Anthologies: Morocco
The Anthologies: Nasrudin
The Anthologies: People
The Anthologies: Quest
The Anthologies: South
The Anthologies: Taboo
The Anthologies: Teaching Stories
The Clockmaker's Box
The Tahir Shah Fiction Reader
The Tahir Shah Travel Reader

Research

Cultural Research

The Middle East Bedside Book

Three Essays

Edited by

Congress With a Crocodile

A Son of a Son, Volume I

A Son of a Son, Volume II

Screenplays

Casablanca Blues: The Screenplay

Timbuctoo: The Screenplay

A REQUEST

If you enjoyed this book, please review it on your favourite online retailer or review website.

Reviews are an author's best friend.

To stay in touch with Tahir Shah, and to hear about his upcoming releases before anyone else, please sign up for his mailing list:

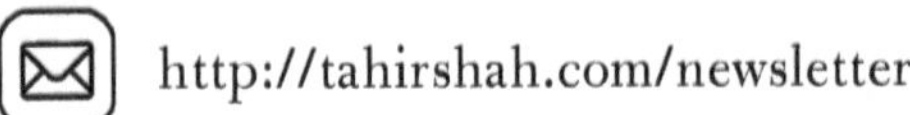

http://tahirshah.com/newsletter

And to follow him on social media, please go to any of the following links:

http://www.twitter.com/humanstew

@tahirshah999

http://www.facebook.com/TahirShahAuthor

http://www.youtube.com/user/tahirshah999

http://www.pinterest.com/tahirshah

https://www.goodreads.com/tahirshahauthor

http://www.tahirshah.com

www.ingramcontent.com/pod-product-compliance
Lightning Source LLC
Chambersburg PA
CBHW030522310726
48979CB00010B/1771/J

* 9 7 8 1 9 1 5 8 7 6 1 2 6 *